JOHA MAKES A WISH
A Middle Eastern Tale

adapted by Eric A. Kimmel
illustrated by Omar Rayyan

Marshall Cavendish Children

For Doris, who makes my wishes come true
—E.A.K.

For my parents, who showed me how to use my wishing stick
—O.R.

Text copyright © 2010 by Eric A. Kimmel
Illustrations copyright © 2010 by Omar Rayyan
All rights reserved
Marshall Cavendish Corporation
99 White Plains Road
Tarrytown, NY 10591
www.marshallcavendish.us/kids

Library of Congress Cataloging-in-Publication Data

Kimmel, Eric A.
Joha makes a wish / by Eric A. Kimmel ; illustrated by Omar Rayyan. — 1st ed.
p. cm.
Summary: An original story, based on the Joha tales of the Arabic-speaking world,
in which a hapless man finds a wishing stick that brings him nothing but bad luck.
Includes an author's note about the history of Joha tales.
ISBN 978-0-7614-5599-8
[1. Wishes—Fiction. 2. Arabs—Fiction. 3. Middle East—Fiction. 4. Humorous stories.] I. Rayyan, Omar, ill. II. Title.
PZ7.K5648Jo 2010
[E]—dc22
2009006334

The illustrations are rendered in watercolor on 140# hotpress paper.
Book design by Anahid Hamparian
Editor: Margery Cuyler
Printed in Malaysia (T)
First edition
1 3 5 6 4 2

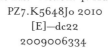

Marshall Cavendish
Children

A Note from the Author

Joha tales are known throughout the Arabic-speaking world. Joha appears as Nasreddin Hoja, the wise fool, in stories from Turkey, Iran, and central Asia. Joha may have worked his way into Western literature as Sancho Panza, Don Quixote's squire and faithful companion. Miguel de Cervantes, the author of *Don Quixote*, could have heard these stories during the six years he spent as a prisoner of the Turks in Algiers.

Joha stories have much to teach about the thin line between wisdom and foolishness. Perhaps that is why Franklin Delano Roosevelt enjoyed listening to them.

This original tale was inspired by "The Answered Prayer," a tale from Yemen. The text of the story can be found in Sharlya Gold and Mishael Maswari Caspi's *The Answered Prayer and Other Yemenite Folktales* (Philadelphia: Jewish Publication Society, 2004). While not specifically a Joha story, it lent itself to Joha's unique blend of wisdom and foolishness.

—E.A.K.

T HE DAY WAS HOT and the road was long. Joha was walking to Baghdad. He stopped to rest in the shadow of a ruined wall. "This shade feels good," Joha said to himself.

Joha leaned against the wall. The old bricks gave way. He fell backward
and landed on top of a sealed jar that had been hidden in the wall.
"I wonder what's in this jar," Joha said. He broke the jar's wax seal.

Inside, he found a stick wrapped up in a parchment scroll. Joha read the scroll's faded letters.

STRANGER,

YOU HAVE FOUND A WISHING STICK.

USE IT WISELY.

IT CAN MAKE YOUR WISHES COME TRUE.

"A wishing stick!" Joha exclaimed. "What will I wish for?" He looked down at his worn-out sandals. "I could use some new shoes."

Joha held the wishing stick in his hand. He closed his eyes. "I wish I had a pair of red leather slippers."

He opened his eyes. He looked down at his feet. He did not have a pair of red leather slippers. He did not have a pair of worn-out sandals, either. His sandals had disappeared!

Joha howled with anger. "What kind of wishing stick is this! I wished for slippers, and now I don't even have sandals. I will have to walk all the way to Baghdad barefoot." Joha glared at the stick in his hand. "You wicked stick! I wish you would disappear."

Instead of disappearing, the stick stuck tight to his hand. This made Joha even angrier. "I lost my sandals because of this stick. Now I can't get rid of it."
He continued down the road to Baghdad, muttering to himself while trying to shake off the stick. "You evil stick! You miserable stick! You unworthy stick!"

"Make way! Make way!" A troop of the sultan's guards trotted past. A little donkey followed behind their horses. Joha hurried to get off the road.

"Those guards are nothing but bullies. It's best to have nothing to do with them," Joha grumbled to himself as the guards rode by. "Still, I wish I had a donkey like that to carry me the rest of the way to Baghdad."

The guards reined in their horses. "Did you hear that?" their leader said. "This fellow wishes he had a donkey to carry. Let's make his wish come true."

"No, no!" cried Joha. "That's not what I said!"

But the guards were having too much fun to hear him. They made Joha bend over while they lifted the donkey onto his back. Down the road they all went, with Joha following behind, carrying the donkey. Everybody on the road stopped to stare. What a sight! They'd often seen a man riding a donkey. How often does anyone get to see a donkey riding a man?

"Hee-haw! Hee-haw!" The donkey brayed and kicked. The poor animal didn't like being carried any more than Joha liked carrying her.

When they arrived at the city gate, the sultan's guards allowed Joha to put the donkey down and go on his way.

"Everything I've said so far has gotten me into trouble. It's the fault of that stick.

I'm not going to say another word to anyone," Joha vowed as he entered the city. He hadn't gone far when he encountered a procession coming down the main street. It was led by the sultan himself.

"Long life to the sultan!" everyone cried as the procession went by.

Everyone except Joha.

The guards noticed his silence. "What's the matter with you? Why won't you wish our sultan a long life?"

"I've had terrible luck with my wishes today," Joha explained. "I'm afraid that if I wish the sultan a long life, something dreadful will happen to him."

The sultan overhead Joha talking. "Don't be afraid," the sultan said. "If you don't want to wish me a long life, you can wish for something else. Wish for something small. That will be enough." The sultan pointed to a tiny wart on the end of his nose. "This wart has been bothering me for a week. I'm tired of it. Wish it to go away."

"I'd rather not," Joha said.

"Perhaps sitting in a dungeon will change your mind?" the sultan asked.

"No," Joha replied. He took a deep breath. Holding tight to the wishing stick, he said, "I wish the wart on the sultan's nose would disappear."

No sooner had he said those words than the tiny wart began to grow. It grew until it was the size of a grape. Then it split in two. The wart kept growing and splitting until it resembled a bunch of purple grapes hanging from the sultan's nose. The guards began to shout.

"This man has bewitched the sultan! Seize him! Off with his head!"

The guards reached for Joha, but he slipped away and ran. The sultan's guards chased him through the winding streets. Joha couldn't run much farther on his aching bare feet. Quickly, he turned down an alley. He saw the entrance to a shop beneath an awning. The shopkeeper was sitting in front reading a book. Joha ran up to him.

"Hide me from the sultan's guards!" he pleaded.

"In here," the old man said. He lifted the lid of a chest. Joha climbed inside. The shopkeeper closed the lid. None too soon! The sultan's guards swarmed into the alley.

"Did you see a man go by?" they asked the shopkeeper. "He carried a stick and wasn't wearing shoes."

The old man shrugged. "I haven't seen anyone like that." The guards moved on.

The shopkeeper helped Joha out of the chest. "What is this all about?" he asked.

Joha described everything that had happened to him from the moment he found the wishing stick in the jar. "All my misfortunes have come from this stick," Joha wailed. "Would that I had never set eyes on it."

"A wishing stick?" the shopkeeper exclaimed. "Now that is something rare. May I see it?"

Joha held out the stick, which was still stuck to his hand.

"No wonder you're having bad luck," the shopkeeper said. "You're holding the stick upside down. The notched end belongs at the top. If the stick is upside down, your wishes will be upside down, too."

"What should I do?" Joha asked.

"Turn the stick around and make a wish."

Joha turned his wrist so that the notched end was at the top. "I wish this stick would fall from my hand," he said.

The stick clattered to the ground. Joha stretched his fingers. He picked up the stick—the right way this time—and said, "I wish I had my old sandals back."

His sandals suddenly appeared on his feet, as dusty and worn as if he had never taken them off.

"This wishing stick is a wonderful thing if you know how to use it," said the old man. "However, before you make any more wishes, you need to go back to the sultan and fix his nose. It is the right thing to do."

Joha agreed. He thanked the old man and walked toward the palace.
He snuck by the guards and crept into the throne room. The sultan was looking in a mirror and clutching his nose. By now his wart looked like a whole harvest of grapes.

"You!" the sultan cried when he saw Joha. "Look what you've done to me!"
"I've come back to fix it," said Joha. He held the wishing stick with the notched end up and said, "I wish the wart on the sultan's nose would disappear."

The wart vanished. The sultan's nose was smooth again.

Everyone congratulated Joha. The sultan was especially pleased. "Is that really a wishing stick? May I see it?" he asked.

Joha handed over his wishing stick.

"I've always wanted to own a wishing stick," the sultan said. "Now I can add this one to my treasures." He gave the wishing stick to one of his servants. "Put this stick in my private chamber. I will be there shortly." He stroked his beard. "What should I wish for?"

"But…," cried Joha. He had never meant to give the sultan his wishing stick.

"I see what you want," the sultan said. "You'd like a reward in return. That's fair. What can I give you? How about a donkey? Yes, a donkey will do." He ordered his guards to bring a donkey from his stables and give it to Joha.

It turned out to be the same donkey that Joha had carried all the way to Baghdad.

"Well, donkey!" Joha said as he climbed onto the donkey's back. "I carried you once. It is only fair that you carry me now." Together they rode away.

As they passed through the streets, Joha asked the donkey, "Donkey, do you think I should go back and tell the sultan he has to hold the stick the right way?"

"Hee-haw!" the donkey brayed.

"I agree," said Joha. "He can figure that out for himself."

But he never did!